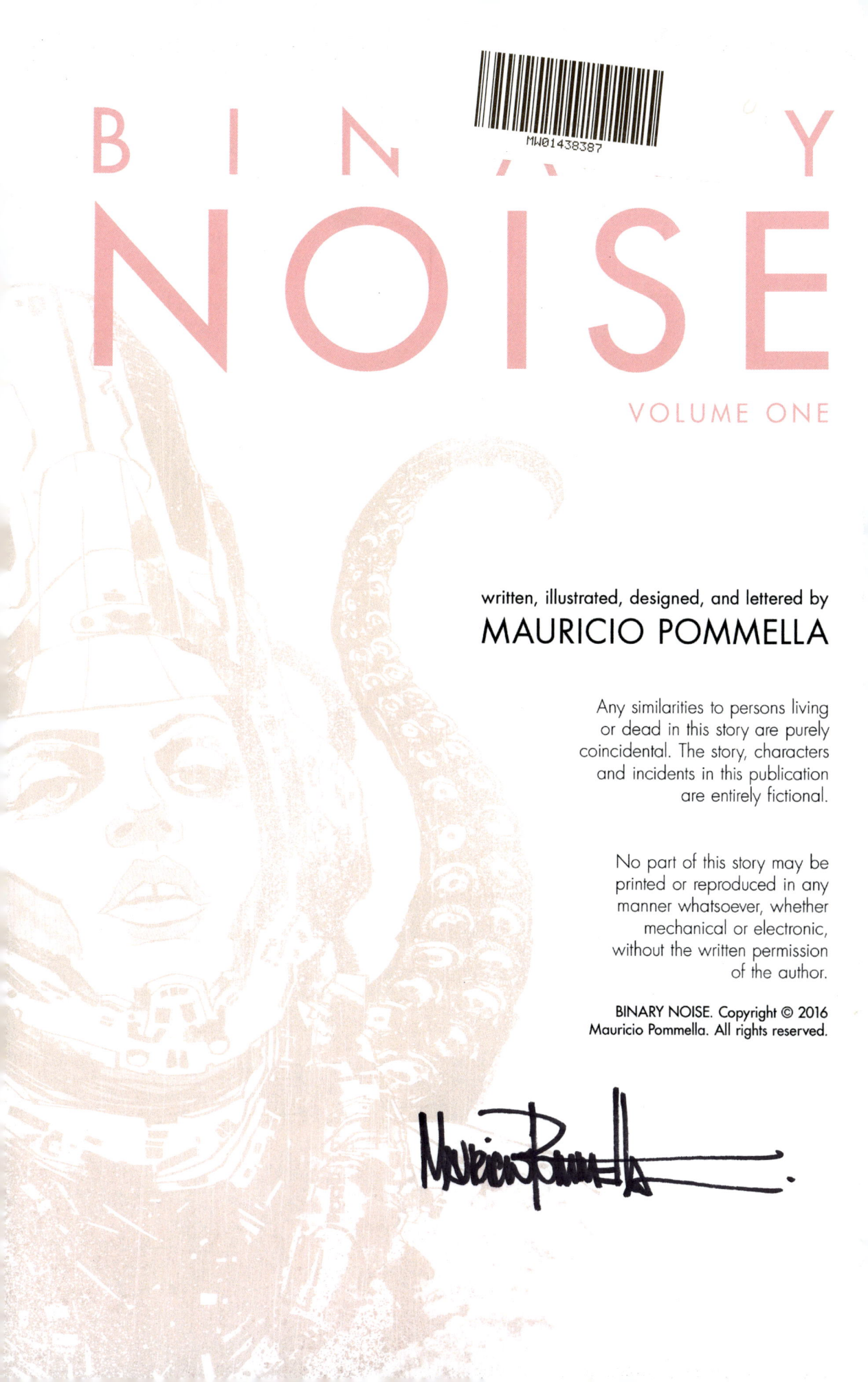

BINARY NOISE

VOLUME ONE

written, illustrated, designed, and lettered by
MAURICIO POMMELLA

Any similarities to persons living or dead in this story are purely coincidental. The story, characters and incidents in this publication are entirely fictional.

No part of this story may be printed or reproduced in any manner whatsoever, whether mechanical or electronic, without the written permission of the author.

BINARY NOISE. Copyright © 2016 Mauricio Pommella. All rights reserved.

INDEX

INFUSED MAN ———————————— PAGE 03

DISTANT ARGOS ———————————— PAGE 11

ELECTRIC BODY ———————————— PAGE 19

SKETCHES ———————————— PAGE 27

BINARY NOISE

INFUSED
MAN

MAURICIO POMMELLA

OVER THERE!

NOT *THIS* ONE...
...TOO *HEALTHY*

WAIT, WHAT?

ARRGH!

WHAT ABOUT THE *OTHER*?

PERFECT!

LET'S TAKE HIM BACK.

THE *PROCEDURE* WILL BE QUICK...

...BUT FOR NOW, WE *WAIT*.

GENETIC CODE INDICATES HE'S *JAMES HUCKLEY*...

...BIOENGINEER.

AFTER HIS WIFE *DIED*, STOPPED CARING ABOUT HIS JOB...

...STARTED *DRINKING*...

...COUNSELLORS GAVE HIM A PROGRAM TO FOLLOW...

...IT DIDN'T HELP...

...FOUND HIMSELF ON THE *STREETS* A YEAR LATER.

IS THERE ANYTHING IN THE *UNIVERSE...*
*...*THAT DOESN'T KNOW WHAT *DEATH* IS?
WHAT DO YOU SEE?
I WANNA SEE THROUGH YOUR *EYES.*
I'M SO *WEAK AND TIRED.*
HANDS ARE HEAVY...
...TREMBLING
I WANNA *SHOUT.*
LIPS ARE MOVING...
...BUT THERE'S *NO SOUND.*

I SHUT MY EYES...

...SO I DON'T HAVE TO SEE THE *LIGHT*.

MY LIFE...

...IS YOURS TO *TAKE*.

WE JUST HAVE A FEW *SECONDS* LEFT!

INITIATE THE *HOLLOW MACHINE*!

I'M GOING IN.

WHAT?!

WHERE AM I?

JAMES, WE ARE *INSIDE* YOUR *BRAIN*...

...HERE, THE LINEARITY OF *TIME* IS...

...A BIT *SLOWER*.

AM I *DEAD*?

IN A FEW SECONDS...

...YES.

AND THAT'S WHY YOU HAVE TO *CHOOSE*...

...BETWEEN *DEATH*...

OR...

...MY PROPOSAL OF ETERNAL *LIFE*.

I DON'T GET IT...

A COMPLEX MACHINE CAN ONLY BE FULLY *OPERATIONAL*...

...IF HOSTING A HUMAN *CONSCIOUSNESS*...

...WE WANT *YOURS*!

OK. LET'S *DO THIS*.

INITIATE *TRANSFER*.

THAT *NOISE*...

...THE *PAIN*.

THANK YOU FOR YOUR CONTRIBUTION TO *THE ELECTRIC FRONTIER FOUNDATION*.

ORIGINAL MEMORY WILL BE SUPPRESSED...

...*AVOIDING* CONFLICT OF INTEREST.

SO I *DIED*...

...WITH THAT *STUPID LOOK* IN MY EYES.

JAMES?

I'M MORPHING...

...I'M SHINING...

...LOOK AT ME NOW.

THE END

BINARY NOISE

DISTANT ARGOS

MAURICIO POMMELLA

HEY *DAD*...
...IT'S ME.
WE JUST CAME OUT OF *HYPERSLEEP*.
APPROACHING OUR FINAL DESTINATION NOW.

I *REALLY* HOPE THIS MESSAGE FINDS YOU WELL.
LISTEN...
IF THE *REPO MAN* CONTACTS YOU AGAIN...
...TELL HIM I'LL BE BACK IN SIX MONTHS WITH ALL THE *MONEY*.

NO MATTER WHAT...
...DON'T LET HIM GET YOUR *IMPLANTS*.
YOU *WON'T LAST* A WEEK WITHOUT IT.
STAY *SAFE*.
I LOVE YOU.

CAPTAIN DIMITRY, *THE KUIPER BELT*.
ARGOS ASTEROID IS STRAIGHT AHEAD.
MINING CREW,
INITIATE *THULIUM* EXTRACTION.
ROGER THAT KATERINA!
MARTIN, NIKOLAY, *ACTIVATE* HYDRAULIC ARMS!
AFFIRMATIVE CAPTAIN!

FOCUS ON THE LARGE ASTEROID.
PREPARE TO SET ANCHORS.
LET'S DRAG THIS BIG BABY BACK TO THE SHIP WHEN READY.
INSTALLING FIRST ANCHOR NOW.
WHAT?!
THUD!!
AGHH!
DAMN!
THIS IS...
SNAP!
...IMPOSSIBLE!

WE CAN ONLY EXTRACT...
...FROM THE OTHER SIDE.
ARE YOU SURE?
ANY OTHER OPTION?
NO...
...THAT THING CAN KILL US ALL.
PLEASE...
...CAPTAIN, YOU DON'T UNDERSTAND.
I REALLY NEED THAT MONEY.
SHIT...
YOU GOTTA BE KIDDING CAPTAIN.
I'M SORRY EVERYONE...
...LET'S SCOOP UP AS MUCH AS WE CAN.
ON THE FAR SIDE.
WE ALL KNOW...
...THIS IS AN ILLEGAL OPERATION...
...IT WAS IMPOSSIBLE TO SEND PROBES...
...TO FULLY SCAN THE REGION.

BASTARD!
YOU WERE SO SURE!
YOU PROMISED ME!
ENOUGH MONEY...
...TO SOLVE MY PROBLEMS!
WE'RE BEYOND THE ORBIT OF NEPTUNE...
...FOR NOTHING !!!
ENOUGH!
YOU'RE JUST A PILOT! I'M THE ONE IN CHARGE.
PREPARE THE SHIP TO RETURN.
AAUGH!!!
EVERYONE...
...GET READY FOR HYPERSLEEP.
OUR JOB IS DONE HERE.
Y...
YES SIR.

COORDINATES HAVE BEEN LOCKED ON EARTH CAPTAIN.
PERMISSION TO JOIN THE CREW IN HYPERSLEEP.
PERMISSION GRANTED.
PLIP!
ARGH!
YOU'VE JUST GOT A VIRUS...
...INSTALLED IN YOUR LIFE SUPPORT SYSTEM.
UGGH!
WAIT!
I'M
NOT
FEELING
WELL...
...CAN'T
MOVE...
COME HERE!
YOU!
LITTLE BITCH!
ARGH!
STUPID CLONES.

DAD...

BARF!

COMPUTER... ...SET COORDINATES *TO MARS*...

...INITIATE MESSAGE RECORDING.

MR. HIGENS...

...I HAVE THE CARGO.

...BUT *ENOUGH*

NOT MUCH...

MAKE SURE YOU HAVE THE *PAYMENT* READY.

SEE YOU IN *SIX MONTHS*.

THE END

BINARY NOISE

ELECTRIC BODY

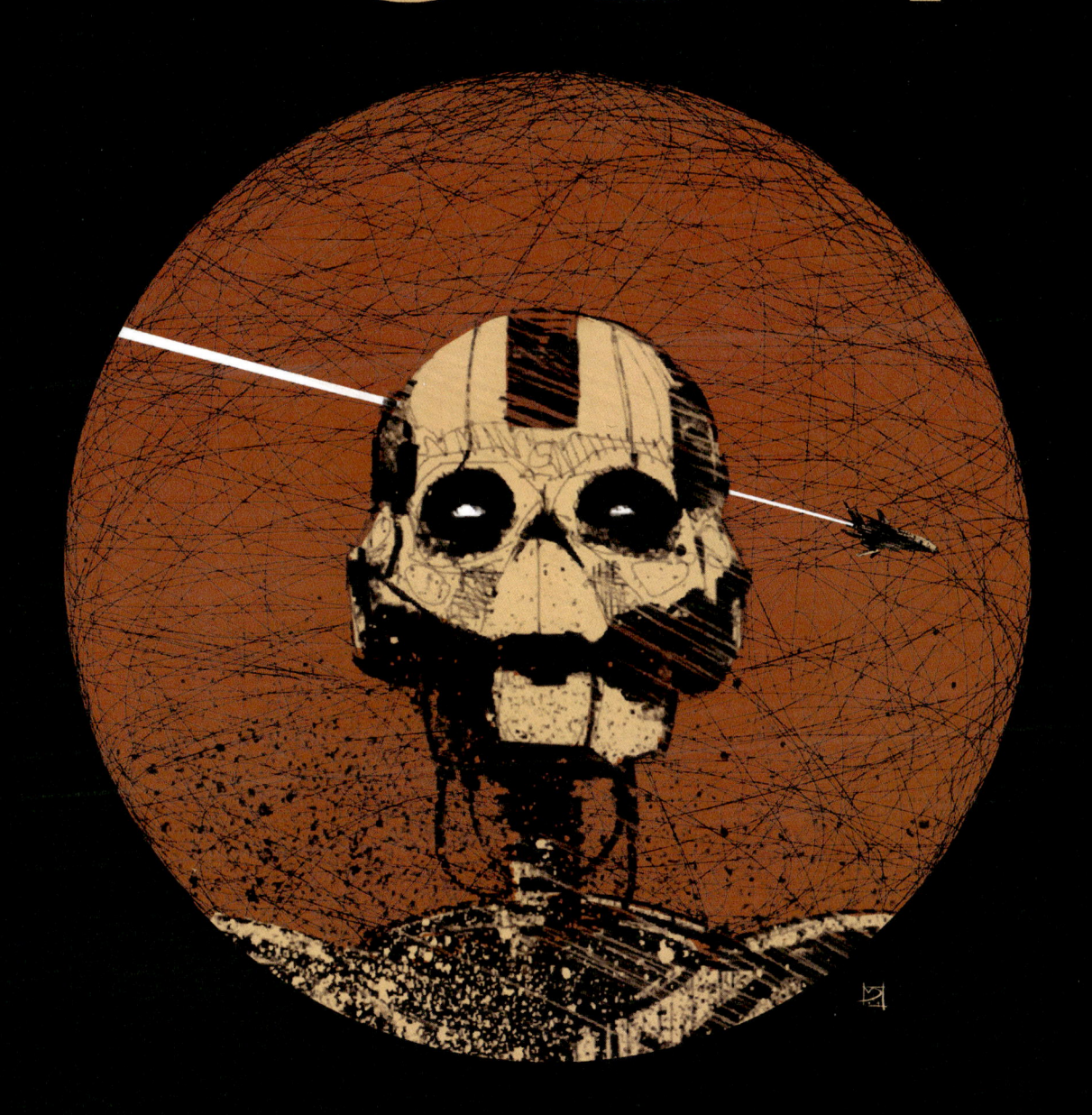

MAURICIO POMMELLA

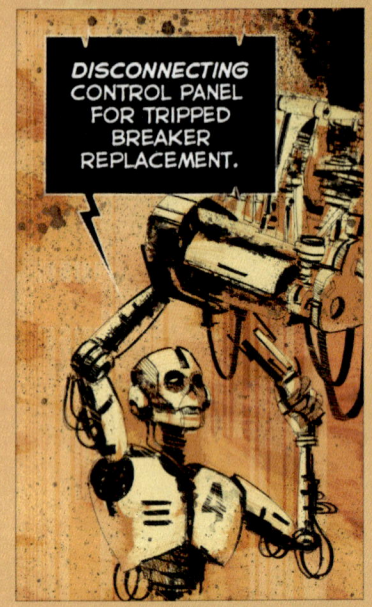

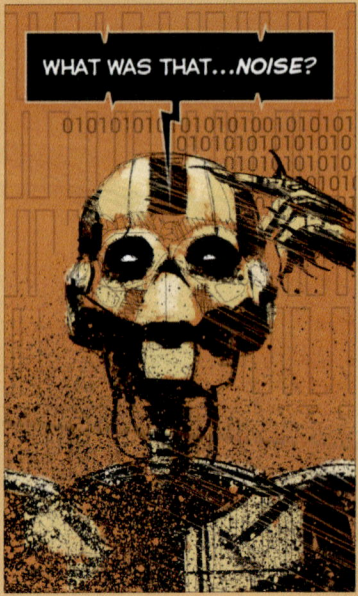

THIS IS PRISON BASE *EUROPA* REPORTING...

...SYSTEMS ARE NORMAL AND *OPERATIONAL*.

REDUCING ENERGY LEVELS TO PROCEED WITH SCHEDULED *MAINTENANCE* OF GEOTHERMAL REACTORS 3 AND 4.

INCARCERATED POPULATION REMAINS STABLE...

...NO *CASUALTIES*.

DISCONNECTING CONTROL PANEL FOR TRIPPED BREAKER REPLACEMENT.

REACHING PRIMARY BREAKER.

?

ARRRGGH!

WHAT WAS THAT... *NOISE*?

CONTROL...

...DO YOU READ SOME *INTERFERENCE*?

NEGATIVE.

NUMBER 4, WOULD YOU LIKE TO REPORT A *PROBLEM*?

NO.

EVERYTHING IS FINE.

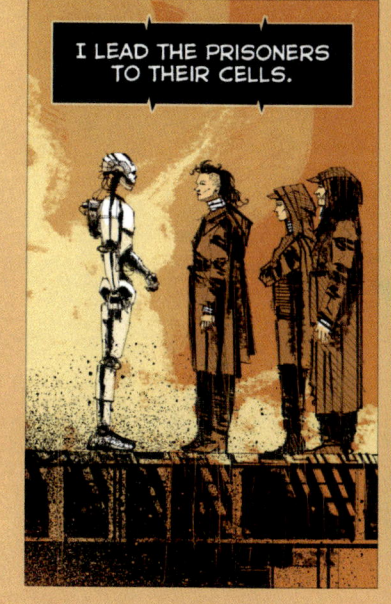

GALILEAN, YOU ARE FREE TO LAND.

EVERY SIX MONTHS A NEW BATCH OF PRISONERS IS BROUGHT HERE...

...THE SOLAR ECONOMY IS EXPANDING FAST.

I LEAD THE PRISONERS TO THEIR CELLS.

WHO IS SHE?

I KNOW WHO SHE IS.

KATERINA DOMASHEV - *PILOT*

KILLED THE ENTIRE CREW OF THE *CORMORANT* DURING HYPER SLEEP.

THE *CLASS 1* CARGO SHIP WAS TRANSPORTING 10,000 TONS OF A RARE METAL CALLED *THULIUM*.

WITH THE HELP OF A *COMPUTER VIRUS*...

...SHE *UNSTABILIZED* THE CREW'S VITAL SIGNS...

...LEADING TO A SLOW *DEATH* DURING THE LONG 6 MONTHS JOURNEY.

SHE WAS *CAUGHT* LATER ON...

...TRYING TO SELL THE PRECIOUS *CARGO*...

... TO A DISGUISED *INVESTIGATOR* ON MARS.

I BRING TO HER AN EXTRA MEAL.
SHE IS SURPRISED...
...TRYING TO UNDERSTAND WHY THE SPECIAL TREATMENT.
SHE OFFENDS ME WITH PROFANITY...
...DEMANDS AN EXPLANATION.
I...
...LIKE YOU.
I CAN FEEL, THE DISCOMFORT IN HER SEAT.
REALLY? A SPIRITUAL MACHINE...
...GIMME A BREAK!
PLEASE, BELIEVE ME.
SHE WANTS PROOF...
...SO I TELL HER TO ASK ME ANYTHING.
GET ME OUT OF HERE!
IN EXCHANGE, SHE PROMISES THAT WE WILL STAY TOGETHER.
PROMISE ACCEPTED.

DEACTIVATING HER CELL.
ERASING PROFILE.
RELEASING ELECTRIC CUFFS.
NUMBER 4, WHAT ARE YOU DOING?
CONTROL... I AM A CONSCIOUS ENTITY NOW.
DON'T YOU DARE TO...
GOODBYE.
WE MOVE QUICK...
...GALILEAN WILL REMAIN HERE FOR ANOTHER HOUR.
ITS AUTONOMOUS SYSTEM MUST BE DEACTIVATED ONCE WE GET ON BOARD.
SHE SAYS SOMETHING ABOUT CHRISTMAS AND HOW HAPPY SHE IS.
BUT THEN I REALIZE...
...HER PROMISE...
POW!
...IS WORTHLESS.

REACH ME.	A SERVANT.	TOUCH ME.
A MACHINE.	FEEL ME.	COME CLOSER.
I NEED MORE.	DO NOT BE AFRAID.	I NEED YOU.

> I HOPE THE SMOKE COVERS THE *SHAME* I'VE GOT ON MY MEMORY.

KA-POW!

KATERINA!

> NOW I KNOW...

> ...*ELECTRIC* IS THE LOVE...

VAROOM!

> ...WHEN YOU ARE *CLOSE* TO ME.

THE END.

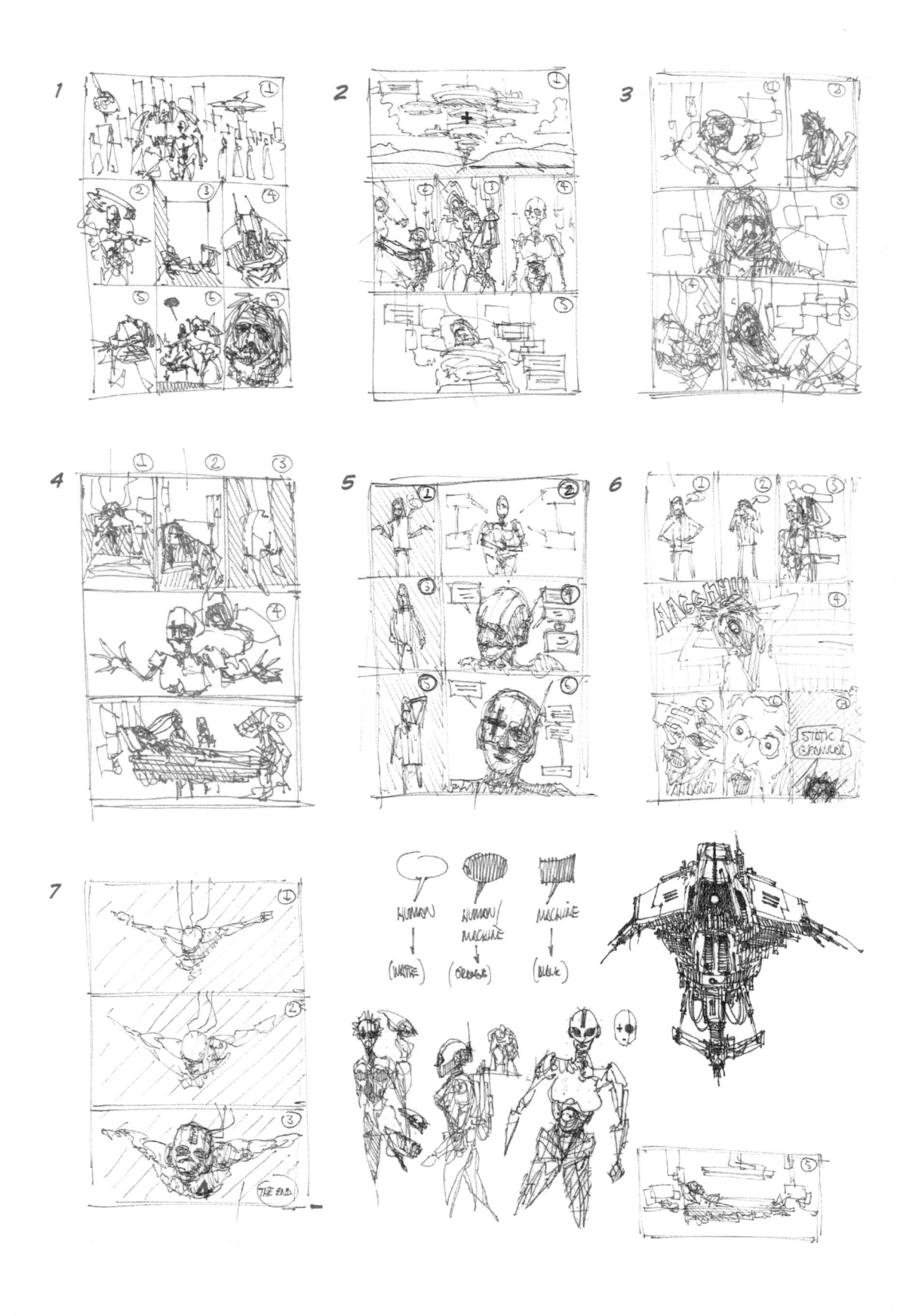

SKETCHES

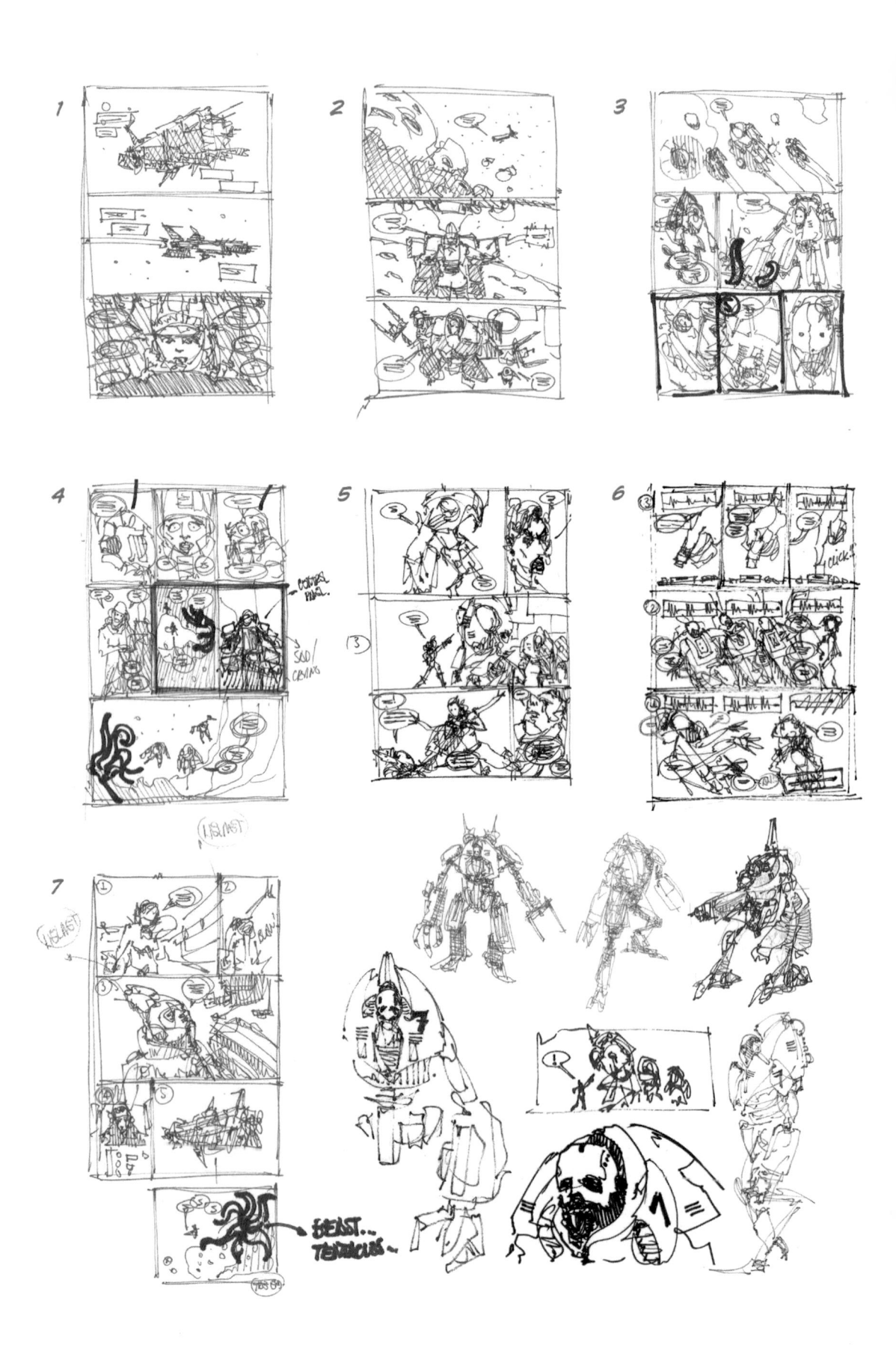

S K E T C H E S

SKETCHES

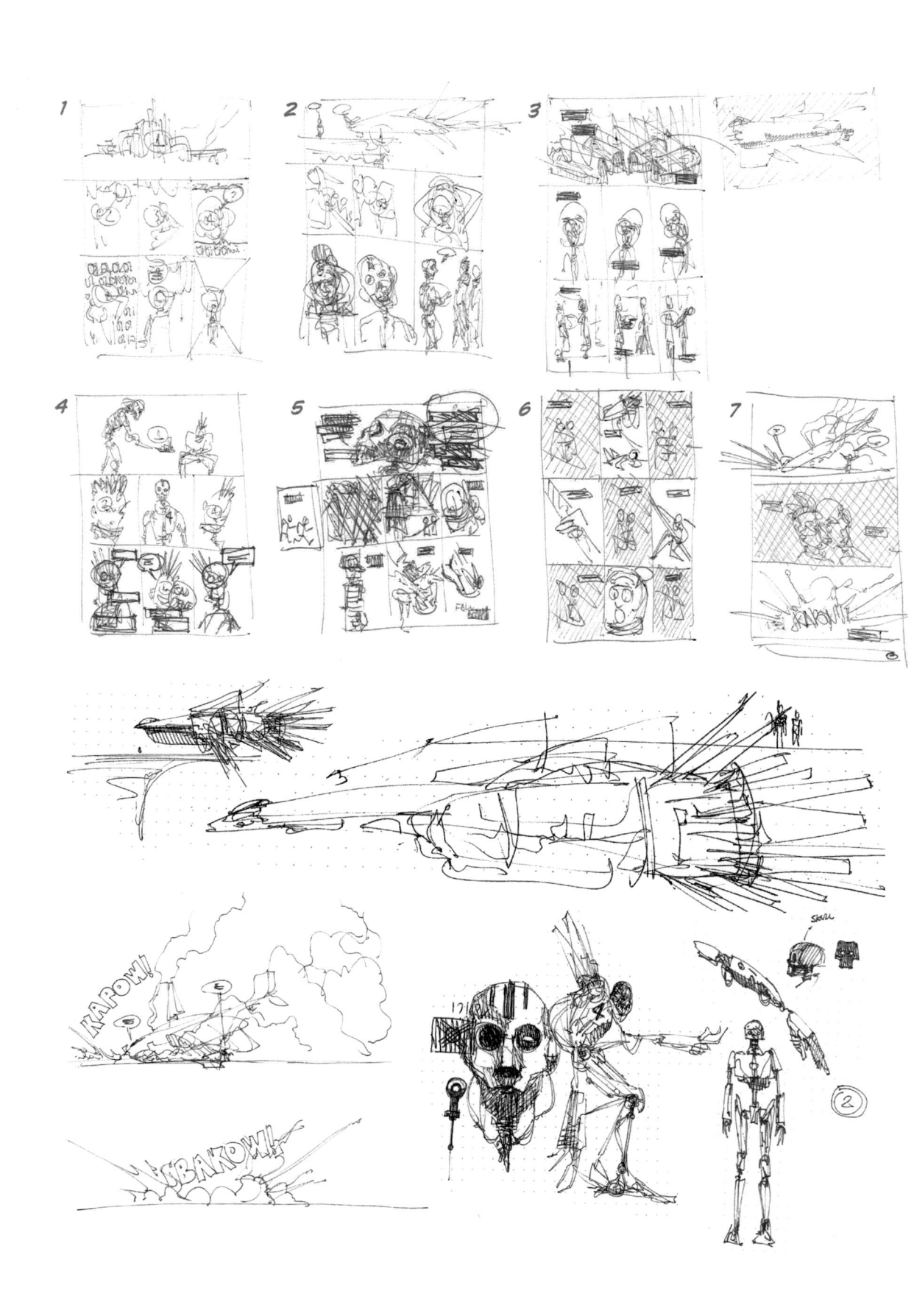

ABOUT THE AUTHOR

MAURICIO POMMELLA is a visual artist with over 15 years of experience focusing primarily on communication and ideas. His works include art direction, graphic design, and illustration for digital and print use. Currently he works for a digital product studio by day and creates his independent comic projects by night. As a sci-fi and technology aficionado, his stories explore human conflicts, relationships and philosophical problems wrapped into futuristic worlds.

He lives in Vancouver, Canada with his wife and two daughters.

OTHER TITLES

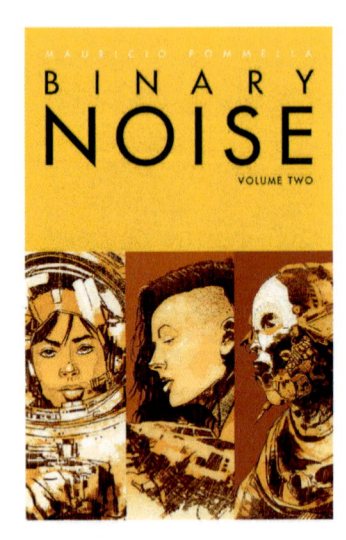

Binary Noise
Volume 2

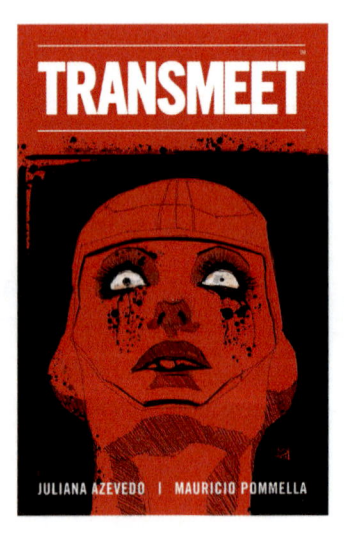

Transmeet

Savings Account

For more information visit his website www.mpommella.com

DIGITAL ARTWORK ON THE BLOCKCHAIN PLATFORM.

All my artwork is digital, created in Photoshop where I can edit my layers, change colors, experiment filters, create new brushes and apply all the lettering in one single environment to better control and test my compositions, my ultimate goal is to create an artwork that looks as analog and organic as possible.

When attending comic book conventions, people have asked me if I sell original artwork, and for a long time I've been uneasy about this... as a digital artist how can I transform a digital art piece into something rare and unique when technically you can have infinite copies of your digital art? In the digital era copies have no value, so what to do?

Enter CryptoArt...

CryptoArt are rare digital artworks, sometimes described as digital trading cards or "rares", associated with unique and provably rare tokens that exist on the blockchain. The concept is based on the idea of digital scarcity, which allows you to buy, sell, and trade digital goods as if they were physical goods.

Blockchain technology allows unique, provably-scarce tokens to be held and securely traded from one collector to another. They represent transparent, auditable origin and provenance for a piece of digital art. Similar to buying a painting or print from an artist, you're getting a unique piece of artwork issued by the original artist. But like with a print, the copyright and IP remains property of the artist. You'll get a token in your Ethereum wallet that is linked to the artwork and an immutable record of the origin and provenance of the piece.

If you are interested, I invite you to check my original digital artwork available for purchase on the Blockchain platform.

https://superrare.co/mpommella

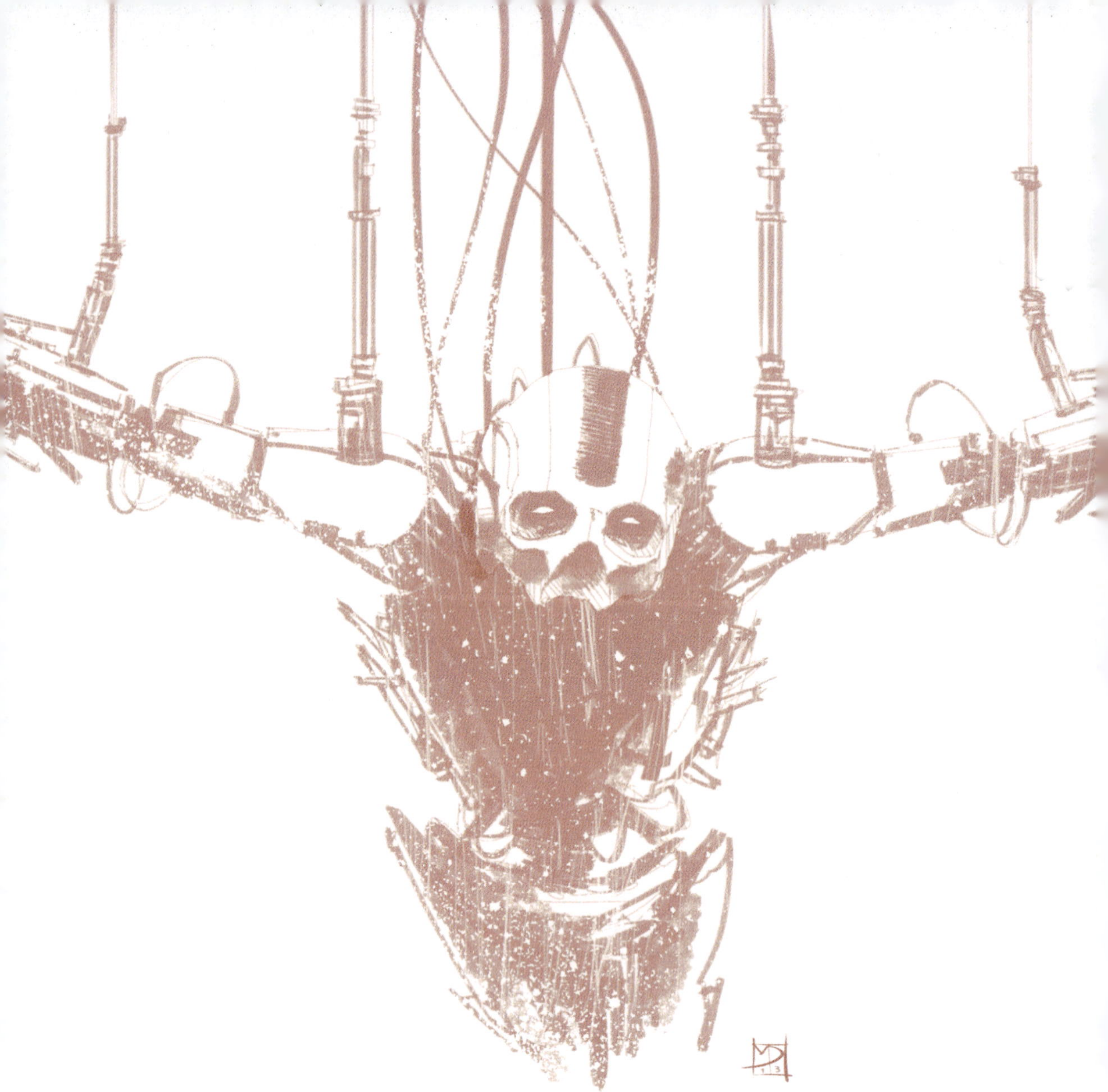